Big Papa
and the
TIME MACHINE

Big Papa and the TIME MACHINE

Story by **Daniel Bernstrom**   Pictures by **Shane W. Evans**

HARPER

An Imprint of HarperCollinsPublishers

Big Papa and the Time Machine

Text copyright © 2020 by Daniel Bernstrom

Illustrations copyright © 2020 by Shane W. Evans

All rights reserved. Manufactured in China.

No part of this book may be used or reproduced in any
manner whatsoever without written permission except in the case
of brief quotations embodied in critical articles and reviews. For
information address HarperCollins Children's Books, a division of
HarperCollins Publishers, 195 Broadway, New York, NY 10007.

www.harpercollinschildrens.com

ISBN 978-0-06-246331-9

The artist used patience, skill, mixed media, pen,
alkyd paint, and digital media tools to create this book.

19 20 21 22 23 SCP 10 9 8 7 6 5 4 3 2 1

❖

First Edition

To those who taught me how to be brave:
Vodes (or Papa), Edsel, Mitch, and Keith
—D.B.

Thank you, God, for the strength to see this
vision through. I dedicate this book to ALL the
Evans, Ciminesi, Allen, Clark, and Eastwood boys
and men, to Warren, Jackie, Paul, Garie Senior,
Joseph, and Olu, to the fathers, uncles, grands,
and greats—we love you, I love you, be brave.
—S.W.E.

I won't never forget that September time when I didn't want to go to school and Big Papa came in his time machine to take us way, way back.

"Do I have to go to school?"

"Yes," Big Papa said.

"I just wanna go home and watch TV."

"You scared," Big Papa said.

"I'm scared I'll miss you."

He turned the key and the engine revved. "I think it's time I showed you somethin' a long time ago."

Little Rock, Arkansas, 1952

We took Big Papa's time machine to a long time ago.

"Big Papa, why that silver-haired lady holdin' that boy tighter than tight?"

"He was leavin' home," Big Papa said. "Needed to find him a job where he could eat fried fish every night."

"Big Papa? That you?"

"Yes," Big Papa said.

"You left your mama!"

"Yes," Big Papa said.

"Was you scared?"

"Scared to death," Big Papa said. "Didn't have no job. Didn't have no money or place to stay."

"But I thought you was never scared."

"No, been scared lots of times," Big Papa said.
"But sometimes you gotta lose the life you
have if you ever gonna find the one you want.

That's called being brave."

We took our time machine to when Big Papa worked in the sky, on top of tall buildings wrapped in coats of smoke and ash.

"You couldn't wear a white shirt back then," Big Papa said. "If you did, it'd be black by the end of the day. All that soot in the air."

"You was so high up. Wasn't you scared?"

"Oh, I was scared," Big Papa said. "Cars looked like toys. And the wind would blow so hard, you think it'd carry you right away."

"Why'd you work up so high?"

"I couldn't stand to stay on the ground," Big Papa said. "Sometimes you gotta walk with giants if you ever gonna find out what you made of.

That's called being brave."

CHICAGO, 1957

We took our time machine to when Big Papa sat by himself in some boogie-bluesy club.

"Hmmm-mmmm," Big Papa said. "Hear those trumpets and them saxophones? They still make my bones wanna swim."

"But why you not dancin'?"

"You see that angel dancin' in a pink dress?" Big Papa said. "Your nana, hmmm-mmmm, she stole my heart with that pink dress."

Then Big Papa jumped into the crowd, and his feet and arms swam with Nana's. And they danced and danced and danced. And Nana held Big Papa tighter than tight.

"I thought you was scared?"

"I tell you, I was scared," Big Papa said. "But sometimes you gotta jump in an ocean of scared if you ever gonna dance with an angel.

That's called being brave."

CHICAGO, 1986

We took our time machine to the day a sad girl left a baby in Big Papa's arms.

"I'm that baby?"

"Yes," Big Papa said. "Your mama left you here for a while."

"But she never came back."

"No," Big Papa said. "She never came back."

"Was you scared?"

"You was so little and I was so old."

"I'm sorry I made you scared."

Big Papa hugged me tighter than tight.

"Sometimes you gotta love the unexpected if you ever gonna find love at all.

That's called being brave."

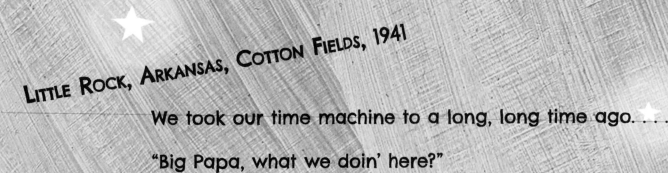

We took our time machine to a long, long time ago. . . .

"Big Papa, what we doin' here?"

A boy who looked just like Big Papa scratched letters on a piece of thin paper.

"Big Papa, is that you?"

Big Papa held my hand tighter than tight. "Just watch."

"What you doin' with that paper?" said a man.

"I'm doin' school."

The man pulled a fistful of cotton from his pocket. "See this cotton, and see that field? Look at it. This is your school."

The man took Little Papa's school paper and ripped it up.

"Give up school, son. Work, that's all you ever gonna do," he said. "That's all we ever can do."

"Did you ever go back to school?"

"No," Big Papa said.

"Does being scared ever go away?"

"No," Big Papa said.

"You scared right now?"

"Big Papa, you scared?"

"Mmmm-hmmm,"
Big Papa said.

"Why you scared?"

"I'm scared you growin' up too fast,"
Big Papa said. "And I already miss you."

I hugged Big Papa tighter than tight.
"But that's called being brave?"

"Yes," Big Papa said.
"That's called being brave."

A note from the author:

Unlike the boy in this story, I grew up not knowing my grandfather. I met him for the first time when I was eighteen. Since I was adopted and raised by a different family, I grew up knowing very little about my history. It was my grandfather—or Papa, as he liked to be called—who taught me my African American story, a story of small displays of courage fueled by a heart full of love. That is to say, bravery.

Year after year, when I visited my biological father in Chicago, I stayed with Papa and Nana in their small brick house on Chicago's South Side. Papa was a storyteller. He would sit and tell story after story, occasionally pausing with a mmmm-hmmm just to reflect, as if he were reliving the whole of his story in a single sound.

My favorite memories with Papa were when he took me driving—always to find some fried chicken or some fried fish. And as he drove around, pointing out the buildings he worked on as a brickmason, Papa would slip in small stories of ordinary courage. He told me how he worked extra jobs to save up money to buy his first car—a 1952 Ford. He told me how he left his family and the South to find work in Chicago. How he lived with twelve other men in a single studio apartment because that's all they could afford. And yes, Papa drove all twelve of them to work in his car!

Other stories came later, when I would call Papa on the phone and he would tell me more of his story: how he met Nana while dancing in the club; how he and Nana couldn't have any children of their own; and how they had adopted my father.

The stories in this book are my papa's, and though some details have been changed, I have tried to preserve the way he told them as best I could. With *Big Papa and the Time Machine*, I wanted to tell my African American story: the story of my journey with Papa driving in and out of time itself as Papa would spin tales of love, loss, courage, and doing brave things even when one is most afraid.

Papa never got to see this book. He passed shortly after I began writing it. And though Papa is gone, I still feel him with me. Whenever I miss him, it's as if, when I open this book, I'm sitting beside my papa as we are driving through Chicago, talking to each other once again.

—Daniel Bernstrom

A note from the illustrator:

To the readers, listeners, and viewers of *Big Papa and the Time Machine*: I hope that you enjoy all the elements of this book. When I first received this story, I immediately saw the challenge at hand. How does one see the past, the present, and the future all in one story? And what is courage? With every line of art, there is a story—just as there is a story in every word. Lines, colors, and marks are a language all their own. Our family lineage is our family story—that line holds us together. Those who have "sent" this line forward to us make us who we are.

When Big Papa, his grandson, and their time machine first appeared in my lines, I began to see the potential in us all. And the courage. Courage is the culmination of the hopes, dreams, and fears of those who choose to love us. Whether we know it or not, our families face decisions that create the paths for us.

Life presents us with a vast number of choices. This book shows that whether our stories are sad or joyful, LOVE will prevail and keep us going through it all. Bravo to everyone who helped to make this book a reality, and to those who encouraged each line and each word.

—Shane W. Evans